# Tall
# Tilly

by Jillian Powell

illustrated by Tim Archbold

Evans

Tilly was growing taller
every day.

She was taller than
all her friends.

She was the tallest girl
in her class.

She was too tall for
her clothes.

She was too tall for her bed.

She was too tall for the bath.

She was even too tall for Ben,
the boy she liked in class!

Worst of all, Tilly wanted
to be a ballerina.

But she was too tall.

Tilly hated it.

She wanted to be small and dainty, like her best friend, Molly.

Then Tilly's teacher had
an idea.

She made Tilly Sports Captain.

Tilly was so tall that she
scored lots of goals for the
basketball team...

...and she saved lots of goals for the football team.

She was so tall she won
every running race.

She jumped the highest
high jumps.

She jumped the longest
long jumps.

Everyone cheered for her.

# Tilly loved being tall after all!

Why not try reading another ZigZag book?

**Dinosaur Planet**     ISBN: 0 237 52667 0
by David Orme and Fabiano Fiorin

**Tall Tilly**     ISBN: 0 237 52668 9
by Jillian Powell and Tim Archbold

**Batty Betty's Spells**     ISBN: 0 237 52669 7
by Hilary Robinson and Belinda Worsley

**The Thirsty Moose**     ISBN: 0 237 52666 2
by David Orme and Mike Gordon

**The Clumsy Cow**     ISBN: 0 237 52656 5
by Julia Moffatt and Lisa Williams

**Open Wide!**     ISBN: 0 237 52657 3
by Julia Moffatt and Anni Axworthy

# Hamish Finds Himself

First published 2005
Evans Brothers Limited
2A Portman Mansions
Chiltern St
London W1U 6NR

British Library Cataloguing in Publication Data
Powell, Jillian
    Hamish finds himself. – (Zig zag)
    1. Children's stories – Pictorial works
    I. Title
    823.9'14 [J]

ISBN 023752953X
13-digit ISBN (from 1 January 2007) 9780237529536

Printed in China by WKT Company Ltd

Series Editor: Nick Turpin
Design: Robert Walster
Production: Jenny Mulvanny
Series Consultant: Gill Matthews

ZIG ZAG

# Hamish Finds Himself

by Jillian Powell

illustrated by Belinda Worsley

Evans

Hamish was the youngest in his family.

Sometimes that was fun.

But it wasn't always fair.
Hamish never had anything new.
He always had old things.

He had Ben's old computer.

He had Tom's old bike.

He even had Ben's old bed,
when Ben grew too big for it.

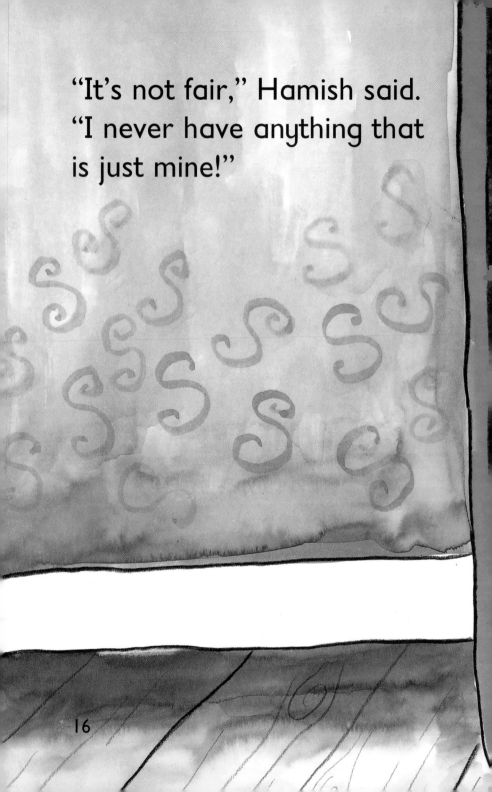

"It's not fair," Hamish said. "I never have anything that is just mine!"

So he went out to
find something that
was just his.

17

First, he found a feather.

But the feather belonged to
a bird.

Then he found a shell.

But the shell belonged to
a snail.

21

Then, he found a ball.

But the ball belonged to
a dog first.

"I'll never find anything that is just mine!" Hamish said.

Then Hamish saw something.

26

He did a handstand.
Then he did
a cartwheel.

29

Hamish had found something
that was just his!

31

Why not try reading another ZigZag book?

**Dinosaur Planet**          ISBN: 0 237 52667 0
by David Orme and Fabiano Fiorin

**Tall Tilly**          ISBN: 0 237 52668 9
by Jillian Powell and Tim Archbold

**Batty Betty's Spells**     ISBN: 0 237 52669 7
by Hilary Robinson and Belinda Worsley

**The Thirsty Moose**     ISBN: 0 237 52666 2
by David Orme and Mike Gordon

**The Clumsy Cow**     ISBN: 0 237 52656 5
by Julia Moffatt and Lisa Williams

**Open Wide!**     ISBN: 0 237 52657 3
by Julia Moffatt and Anni Axworthy

**Too Small**     ISBN 0 237 52777 4
by Kay Woodward and Deborah van de Leijgraaf

**I Wish I Was An Alien**     ISBN 0 237 52776 6
by Vivian French and Lisa Williams

**The Disappearing Cheese**     ISBN 0 237 52775 8
by Paul Harrison and Ruth Rivers

**Terry the Flying Turtle**     ISBN 0 237 52774 X
by Anna Wilson and Mike Gordon

**Pet To School Day**     ISBN 0 237 52773 1
by Hilary Robinson and Tim Archbold

**The Cat in the Coat**     ISBN 0 237 52772 3
by Vivian French and Alison Bartlett

**Pig in Love**     ISBN 0 237 52950 5
by Vivian French and Tim Archbold

**The Donkey That Was Too Fast**     ISBN 0 237 52949 1
by David Orme and Ruth Rivers

**The Yellow Balloon**     ISBN 0 237 52948 3
by Helen Bird and Simona Dimitri

**Hamish Finds Himself**     ISBN 0 237 52947 5
by Jillian Powell and Belinda Worsley

**Flying South**     ISBN 0 237 52946 7
by Alan Durant and Kath Lucas

**Croc by the Rock**     ISBN 0 237 52945 9
by Hilary Robinson and Mike Gordon